Bo and the Little Lie

by Elliott Smith

illustrated by Subi Bosa

Cicely Lewis, Executive Editor

Lerner Publications ◆ Minneapolis

A Letter from Cicely Lewis

Dear Reader,

This series is about a boy named Bo and his grandfather in the barbershop called the Buzz. The barbershop has always been the hub of the Black community. In a world where Black voices are often silenced, it is a place where these voices can be heard.

I created the Read Woke challenge for my students so they can read books that reflect the diversity of the world. I hope you see the real-life beauty, richness, and joy of Black culture shine through these pages.

—Cicely Lewis, Executive Editor

TABLE OF CONTENTS

Bo's World

Hi, I'm Bo. I like basketball,
science, and flying in airplanes.
This is my grandpa, Roger.
I call him Pop-Pop.

We live upstairs from the Buzz. It's the barbershop Pop-Pop owns.

I like hanging out with my friends Silas, Shawn, and Zuri.

CHAPTER 1
A Favor

Back and forth, back and forth walked Bo in his room. He grabbed his baseball glove. Then he snagged a jump rope. Next up, swim trunks. He jammed it all into his backpack.

Silas had invited him to go to MegaPark. It had sports fields and waterslides. He pictured himself catching a fly ball in front of a cheering crowd.

Bo ran downstairs to the barbershop. He jumped into the empty chair next to his grandfather and spun around. "I'm ready to go!" he shouted.

“Before you go, I need you to do me a favor,” Pop-Pop said. He grabbed an envelope from the ledge under a mirror. “I need you to put this letter in the mailbox,” he said.

Bo grabbed the letter. It was addressed to City Electric.

“Sure thing, Pop-Pop,” Bo said. “See you later!”

City Electric

OPEN

Bo burst out the door. He thought about Pop-Pop's letter. But the mailbox was in the other direction from Silas's house. *I'll mail it later*, he thought. It was MegaPark time!

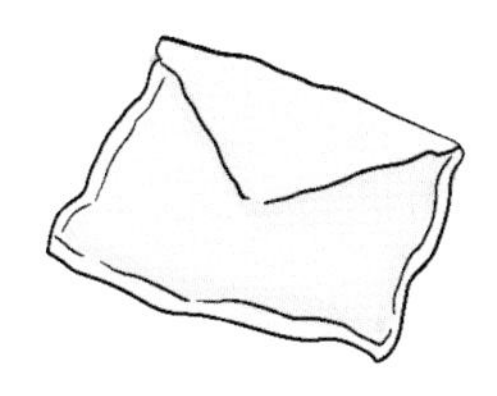

CHAPTER 2

The Lie

A few days later, Bo was putting snacks in the mini fridge. He was still thinking of all the fun he'd had at MegaPark. He couldn't wait to go back!

"Bo!" Pop-Pop called as he shaved a man's beard. "Did you remember to mail my letter?"

"What letter?" Bo asked.

"The electric bill I gave you to put in the mailbox," Pop-Pop said.

Cola
Cola
PoP!
Pop!
Pop!
PoP!

Bo panicked. "Uh . . . yeaaah," he said. He thought about the letter sitting at the bottom of his bag. "I sure did."

"Okay," Pop-Pop said. His face didn't look as if he believed Bo. "I'm glad you did. Because if you didn't, the lights in the shop would go out."

Bo's stomach dropped. He started sweating. "Be right back," he said.

Bo ran up to his room and found his bag. He yanked everything out. The letter was gone. He must have lost it at MegaPark!

LARON
BLAZE
SNEAKERS

Should I tell Pop-Pop? Bo wondered. If he did, he'd get in trouble for lying. He paced back and forth in his room.

Maybe someone had found the letter and mailed it. That's what he would have done if he'd found a letter like that. Bo felt a little bit better. But just a little.

CHAPTER 3

Lights Out

It was a busy Saturday at the Buzz. Bo sat in the waiting area, reading a comic book.

Suddenly, the lights flickered. Bo looked up. Had anyone else seen that? Then, *Blip!* The shop was completely dark.

SPARKS

Pop-Pop came over to Bo. “Bo, did you really mail my letter?” he asked.

Bo knew he was busted. “No,” he said quietly. “I forgot to mail it, and then I lost it at MegaPark. I didn’t want to get in trouble.”

“Bo, lying is never the right choice,” Pop-Pop said. “Lies always come back to hurt you or someone else.”

BUZZ

Jorge
CITY ELECTRIC

A moment later, the lights came back on. A smiling man walked in. He wore a blue shirt with a "City Electric" patch on it.

"Bo, meet Jorge," Pop-Pop said. "He's my friend from City Electric."

Bo's jaw dropped.

"I knew you didn't mail my letter," Pop-Pop explained. "I checked my account last week. So I had Jorge come over and turn off the lights from outside to teach you a little lesson."

“You’re lucky your grandfather double-checked his bill,” Jorge said. “It can cost a lot of money to turn your lights back on.”

“I’m sorry, Pop-Pop,” Bo said. “I won’t tell any more lies.”

“I hope not,” Pop-Pop said. “But you’ll have time to think about it. You’re on sweeping duty for a month.”

Bo hugged Pop-Pop and grabbed the broom. He was happy to fix his mistake. Even if it meant sweeping hair.

Buzz

About the Author

Elliott Smith has been writing stories ever since he was a kid. This love of writing led him first to a career as a sports reporter. Now, he has written more than 40 children's books, both fiction and nonfiction. Smith lives just outside Washington, DC, with his wife and two children. He loves watching movies, playing basketball with his kids, and adding to his collection of Pittsburgh Steelers memorabilia.

About the Illustrator

As a child, Subi Bosa drew pictures all the time, in every room of the house—sometimes on the walls. His mother still tells everyone, "He knew how to draw before he could properly hold a pencil."

In 2020, Subi was awarded a Mo Siewcharran Prize for Illustration. Subi lives in Cape Town, South Africa, creating picture books, comics, and graphic novels.

Lerner Publications Company
An imprint of Lerner Publishing Group, Inc.
241 First Avenue North
Minneapolis, MN 55401 USA

For reading levels and more information, look up this title at www.lernerbooks.com.

Main body text set in Mikado 24/41. Typeface provided by Hannes von Doehren.

Library of Congress Cataloging-in-Publication Data

Names: Smith, Elliott, 1976- author. | Bosa, Subi, illustrator.
Title: Bo and the little lie / by Elliott Smith ; illustrated by Subi Bosa.
Description: Minneapolis : Lerner Publications, [2023] | Series: Bo at the Buzz (Read woke chapter books) | Audience: Ages 6-9. | Audience: Grades 2-3. | Summary: "Bo's grandfather asks him to mail an important letter. But when Bo forgets to mail it, he lies to his grandfather. Follow along as Bo learns the importance of telling the truth"– Provided by publisher.
Identifiers: LCCN 2022014623 (print) | LCCN 2022014624 (ebook) | ISBN 9781728476162 (lib. bdg.) | ISBN 9781728486307 (pbk.) | ISBN 9781728481432 (eb pdf)
Subjects: CYAC: Honesty—Fiction. | African Americans—Fiction. | LCGFT: Fiction.
Classification: LCC PZ7.1.S626 Bol 2023 (print) | LCC PZ7.1.S626 (ebook) | DDC [Fic]—dc23

LC record available at https://lccn.loc.gov/2022014623
LC ebook record available at https://lccn.loc.gov/2022014624

Manufactured in the United States of America
1 - CG - 12/15/22